Furry FRIENDS

Peril in Paris

FURRY FRIENDS

Peril in Paris

HOLLY WEBB

Illustrated by Clare Elsom

SCHOLASTIC

Scholastic Children's Books
An imprint of Scholastic Ltd
Euston House, 24 Eversholt Street, London, NW1 1DB, UK
Registered office: Westfield Road, Southam, Warwickshire, CV47 0RA
SCHOLASTIC and associated logos are trademarks and/or
registered trademarks of Scholastic Inc.

First published in the UK by Scholastic Ltd, 2017

ISBN 978 1407 15434 3

A CIP catalogue record for this book
is available from the British Library.

Printed by CPI Group (UK) Ltd, Croydon, CR0 4YY

Papers used by Scholastic Children's Books are made
from wood grown in sustainable forests.

1 3 5 7 9 10 8 6 4 2

www.scholastic.co.uk

CHAPTER ONE

"Josephine! Josephine! Oh, where are you?"
Sophie crouched next to the little cone-
shaped box tree and peered underneath,
searching for the doorway. But she had to
jump up after a second or two, as a group
of visitors came chattering down the steps.
If she was kneeling there for too long, other

people might wonder what she was looking at, and then they'd lean down and look too, and that would be a disaster.

When Sophie had first discovered that there was a colony of talking guinea pigs living underground at the church of *Sacré Coeur*, she had been sworn to secrecy. Josephine was the first of the guinea pigs she'd met,

a gorgeous, friendly ginger-and-white furball. She had rescued Sophie when she had a fall. The little

guinea pig had been too worried about Sophie to leave her lying there on the grass, and she had broken all the rules about not being spotted by humans to make sure that Sophie wasn't badly hurt. Ever since then, Sophie's new home in Paris had become a fabulous adventure.

"Where on earth can she be?" Sophie wondered. She'd last seen Josephine the day before. Sophie had popped by the gardens of the *Sacré Coeur* on the way home from school, just to say a quick hello before she went to her swimming class. She'd told Josephine that she'd be back today — it was Saturday, they'd have the whole morning to spend together.

That was, if Sophie could ever find her.

The guinea pig family who lived under the gardens were nocturnal – or almost, anyway. Now that she had known them for a few weeks, Sophie had decided that actually they just slept whenever they felt like it. Josephine's uncle Ernest seemed to spend most of his life gently snoozing in his burrow. He always slept tucked up

under a patchwork quilt he'd made himself from scraps of clothes left behind by visitors to the gardens. He had brought it out to show to Sophie, wearing it like a trailing, multi-coloured cloak. With his wild, whirly fur, he'd looked like a tiny magician.

So even though Josephine *ought* to be asleep in her burrow, she could be anywhere. Sophie sighed and sat down on the steps, sinking her chin in her hands. She'd wanted to ask Josephine's advice. Sophie's mum had been working very hard recently, but she'd just finished a big project, and she said she wanted to make up for being busy by having a special Sunday afternoon treat, just her and Sophie. Dan

was going to watch a film with Dad. Sophie was really looking forward to it, though she wasn't sure what they ought to do. She'd been planning to ask Josephine if she had any ideas. The little guinea pig had been living in Paris for a lot longer than Sophie had, after all. She was sure to think of something fun.

"What have you done with Josephine?" a cross little voice demanded.

Sophie glanced down, smiling. Even though Angelique sounded grumpy, Sophie didn't mind. The white guinea pig had been very jealous of Sophie's friendship with her sister, and she had tried to stop Josephine from talking to Sophie. Even though

they were almost
friends now, Sophie
had decided that
Angelique actually
enjoyed being
grumpy.

"I haven't done
anything with her!"
Sophie protested.
"I was looking for her. Are you looking for
her too?"

"Yes," Angelique admitted, folding her
paws across her front. "She ought to be
asleep in the burrow," she added sternly.
"Not outside messing about with you."

"Well, she isn't." Sophie sighed.

"I only came to say hello."

"Hmmm." Angelique tapped her thin pink claws together, and Sophie decided that she looked more worried than cross. "You really don't have any idea where she is?" the white guinea pig asked, almost pleadingly. "She wanders off and I never know where she'll be. One of these days she's going to get herself into trouble on one of your silly adventures!"

"I promise. I would tell you, Angelique, if I knew. Oh! Is that...?" Sophie jumped up and ran towards one of the benches. Angelique dashed after her, the grass on her special disguising hat flying backwards in the wind.

"She's here!" Sophie whispered, as Angelique came puffing towards her.

"She doesn't even have her hat on!" Angelique said disapprovingly. "Josephine, whatever are you doing out here? This is most irregular."

"Josephine, are you all right?" Sophie sat down on the bench and peered underneath, trying not to look too obvious about it. It was a beautiful sunny September day, and the gardens were full of visitors. She didn't want to draw attention to the ginger guinea pig. Josephine didn't answer her. She just lay there, flat on her back, with her little paws sticking up in the air.

"Is she ill?" Sophie asked Angelique worriedly. "Why doesn't she answer?"

"Perhaps she's been eating macarons again," Angelique muttered, gently pulling at one of her sister's paws. "I told her not to. I told her they would upset her stomach. Guinea pigs are not supposed to eat cake! But she never listens."

Sophie thought there was tiny flicker of one of Josephine's eyelids at that, but she couldn't be sure.

"Do you think a macaron would wake her up?" she asked Angelique.

One of Josephine's eyes definitely opened a crack this time, and Angelique pounced and pulled her sister's whiskers. "You're pretending!" she squeaked. "There's nothing wrong with you at all!"

"I never said there was!" Josephine squeaked indignantly. "You let go of my whiskers! Ow! Ow!"

"But why were you lying there like that?" Sophie asked. "We thought you were really ill."

"I'm not ill. . ." Josephine sat up and heaved a dramatic sigh. "I'm bored."

"Bored!" Angelique squeaked. "How can you be bored? Read a book! I'll find you one of Dan's." Sophie's brother Dan had lent Angelique all sorts of books – they were a bit of an odd selection, because only very small books could fit through the door of the burrow. Dan had taken to visiting the second-hand bookstalls on the banks of the River Seine, just to buy titchy burrow-sized books.

"I don't want to read," Josephine muttered, flapping her paws. "I want to *do* something! Something exciting! Nothing exciting ever happens here." She glared around at the perfect emerald grass, the gently splashing fountain, and the huge, glittering white church on the top of the hill. It was beautiful.

"Apart from you, Sophie," Josephine added, resting a pink paw on Sophie's knee. "You were the most exciting thing to happen to me in years. But now I want an adventure. Do you see?"

"I might have known it would be her fault," Angelique said, scowling. "You never wanted adventures before she came."

"Yes, I did! I just never believed that I could have one. It was all about tidying up and nibbling the grass neat and listening to Ernest tell the same stories over and over again. But now I know things . . . I want to go out and explore Paris!"

CHAPTER TWO

Sophie stared at the little guinea pig, frowning. "But you live in Paris... You've lived here for ages. Haven't you explored it all already?"

"Certainly not!" Angelique leaned in between Sophie and Josephine, sternly waving her paw. "We do *not* go exploring! We live here. We might – just occasionally – leave the gardens for the most terribly important reasons, but that's all!" Angelique meant the time that she and Josephine had visited the apartment where Sophie lived. Sophie could see that she still felt a bit guilty about it.

"I don't see that it matters, as long as you're really, really careful," she said. "We didn't let anyone see you, did we?"

"That is not the point," Angelique told her severely. "It was very risky and entirely inadvisable."

"She means it was a bad idea," Josephine explained. "And I think she's entirely wrong. We should know all about Paris, Angelique."

"I do." The white guinea pig stuck her nose in the air. "I have read many guidebooks. They get left behind on benches all the time. I can tell you everything about everywhere in this city."

"But you've never been to any of these places!" Josephine cried. "It's not the same."

Angelique stared at her for a moment, and then her shoulders sagged and she stared down at the path. "Perhaps..." she admitted. "But I like it here, Josephine. I don't want to go anywhere new."

Josephine stood up, planting her paws on her hips. Her whiskers fanned out and her eyes sparkled. She looked taller, Sophie thought. Suddenly she was every

inch an explorer guinea pig, ready for any
adventure.

"So what
are you going
to do?" Sophie
asked. "Where
will you go?"

Josephine's
whiskers
drooped a little. "I'm not sure." Then she
nodded determinedly. "Perhaps I'll go
parachuting. I could skydive off the top of
the *Tour Eiffel*."

"No!" yelped Angelique and Sophie
together.

"I don't think guinea pigs are designed

for parachuting," Sophie said quickly.

Angelique nodded. "We are not very aerodynamic."

"Hmf. Well, then, I shall learn to drive a racing car." Josephine glared. "I suppose you're going to say that I can't do that, either?"

Sophie bit her lip. "I don't think you could reach the pedals. I don't think even I could. Josephine, I know it's not as exciting as parachutes or racing cars, but would you like to come on an adventure with me? Mum says we can do anything I like tomorrow. It's my special treat, because she says she's hardly seen me in weeks."

"Oh!" Josephine nodded delightedly. "Of course I would. But shouldn't it be just you and your mother?"

Sophie stopped for a moment, thinking. Maybe Josephine was right. Then she shook her head. "No. Mum loves Paris. She's so excited about living here again. If she knew that you'd never had the chance to explore the city, she'd want you to come with us. I know she would."

"Then yes, yes!" Josephine squeaked. "Angelique, are you sure you won't come too? Just a little adventure? A tiny, tiny one?"

"No, thank you," Angelique said primly. "I shall stay here and sleep, so that I'm

ready to do our proper work tomorrow
night."

Sophie looked guilty, but Josephine laid
a tiny paw on her arm. "Just ignore her,
Sophie. Sisters. . ." She leaned over and
planted a tiny kiss on Angelique's pink
nose. "She's so bossy. So, tomorrow! What
shall we do? If you're sure we can't go
skydiving."

"I'm sure. Mum would definitely say no
to that."

Angelique jumped up! "Oh! I know. And
it's a way that you can see lots of the city.
The guidebooks say it is UNMISSABLE."

"What is it?" Sophie asked excitedly.

"A boat trip down the River Seine. It

starts from near the *Tour Eiffel*, and you sail past the Louvre, and the church of *Notre-Dame*." Angelique nodded excitedly. "It sounds *magnifique*."

"Oh, yes!" Sophie nodded. "That would be brilliant. I love boats! What do you think, Josephine? Is it adventurous enough?"

Josephine clasped her paws thoughtfully. "Would I, perhaps, be able to drive the boat?"

Sophie and Angelique exchanged glances. "No," Sophie said apologetically. "I don't think so. How could we do that and still keep you a secret? And I don't think they'd let guests drive the boat anyway."

"I suppose. Oh, very well, yes. It isn't quite as adventurous as I'd like, but we can save skydiving for another time."

Sophie crossed her fingers behind her back and nodded. "Will you meet me at the apartment? It might be difficult to explain to Mum why I have to come here first."

"Of course I will." Josephine looked away shyly, scratching the dusty path with her paw. "What sort of time should I arrive? Perhaps . . . breakfast time?"

Sophie giggled, and then carefully turned it into a cough. "Oh, yes. That's a very good idea. It would be awful if we went early and left without you." She knew quite well that Josephine was hoping there would be something delicious for breakfast. She crouched down to hug Josephine and then Angelique. "I'd better go. See you tomorrow!"

The next morning, Sophie was woken by a gentle tapping on the French windows leading from her bedroom out on to the tiny ironwork balcony. Josephine was bouncing up and down outside and waving at her. Sophie hurried to let her in.

"Am I too early?" Josephine asked anxiously. "I didn't mean to wake you. I was so excited about our trip that I woke

up almost at sunrise, and I just couldn't wait any longer."

"Sunrise! Oh, the church must have looked beautiful!" Sophie exclaimed.

"Orange and pink and gold," Josephine agreed, with a happy little sigh. "But now that I have walked all that way I am quite tired, Sophie. And I had to avoid a poodle out on an early-morning walk, and he very nearly gobbled me up. So I am feeling quite faint and exhausted. From the shock, you see." She scurried inside and looked hopefully at Sophie.

"It isn't quite breakfast time yet," Sophie said, picking Josephine up and carrying her back to the bed. "Mum won't be up, and I

know she bought some croissants to warm
up, and *pains au chocolat*."

"Mmmm!" Josephine flumped
backwards on to Sophie's duvet, with an
expression of pure bliss on her furry face.
"Well, I might just manage to wait. If it
isn't *too* long." She sat up and stared happily
round at Sophie's room.

"I'll get dressed," Sophie said, yawning.
"If Mum hears me moving about, she might
decide it's time to get up as well." Sleepily, she
started to pull clothes out of her wardrobe.
Maybe jeans would be nice and warm for
on the river? It was only late September,
but already there was a chill in the air and
the leaves were browning on the trees. She

27

decided on jeans and a fleecy hoodie.

"Ooooh, Sophie, you have a sailor hat! You should wear that!" Josephine said excitedly. "It's perfect for today."

"I don't. . ." Sophie looked puzzled. She only had a couple of winter hats and a cap for the summer. What could Josephine be talking about? Then she smiled. "That's not a hat. I mean, it is, but it's not for wearing. Mum gave it to me — she's had it since she was a little girl. It was the lid from a box of chocolates." She picked up the tiny sailor hat from the top of her bookcase and showed it to Josephine properly. It was beautifully made from soft blue felt, with a white ribbon and a bright red pompom on top. "They used to sell them with chocolate pebbles inside. They were her favourite treat."

"Chocolate pebbles!" Josephine's eyes grew rounder. "If I had chocolate pebbles I could pretend to Angelique that I was collecting them and she wouldn't tell me off! She'd never even know that they were sweeties."

"I'll look out for them," Sophie told her. "But I don't think they sell them in these hats any more. Anyway, the hat's too small for me, but you could wear it, Josephine." She lifted it up and placed it carefully over the little guinea pig's gingery ears. It slipped over to one side, but it was just the right size.

"It's perfect! Very *chic*." She lifted Josephine so she could see into the mirror on the wall.

"Oh, I love it! I will take the greatest care of it, Sophie, I promise. I've only ever worn the grass hat  that Angelique made for me, but this is so smart."

"Sophie?" Mum put her head around the door, and Josephine and Sophie froze. "Oh, you are up! I thought I could hear you. Have you thought about what you might like to do today? I forgot to ask you last night."

"Please can we go on a riverboat trip down the Seine?" Sophie asked. "It's a way to see lots of the nicest bits of Paris, someone told me."

"A boat trip," Mum said slowly. "Yes . . . I suppose so."

"Don't you want to?" Sophie looked at her worriedly.

"Of course I do. I said anything, didn't I?" Mum smiled. "Come on – let's get those croissants warming up."

"Croissants!" There was a tiny squeak in Sophie's ear, and Mum turned round curiously.

"Oh, I mean, croissants, yummy!" Sophie said with a grin. "I'll just get dressed!"

Chapter Three

"Oh, look, look! The river!"

"Ssshhh! Mum will hear you!" Sophie leaned over and whispered into her shoulder bag. She'd told Mum she wanted to bring her purse, and a scarf in case it was chilly – but really the bag was for carrying Josephine.

"I'm sorry, Sophie, I can't help it. It's just so exciting." Josephine peeped out over the edge of the bag, clinging on to the fabric with her little paws. Sophie hoped that to the people passing by, she just looked like a toy. "I never thought it would be so big!"

"It's huge," Sophie agreed. "And so sparkly!" The sun was out and the water glittered as they looked down.

"And there is the *Tour Eiffel* too,"

Josephine said dreamily. "I've heard so much about it, and now I've seen it at last. It was worth that awful journey." She closed her eyes and Sophie could feel her shudder.

"I know it took a while on the Metro, but it wasn't that bad."

"The juddering! The squeals! And so many people, pushing and rushing about. I did not like it at all, Sophie. I was frightened."

"Oh dear, maybe I shouldn't have brought you. Perhaps we should walk back on the way home? But it's a long way, it would probably take us hours. We could walk part of it, so there's not so many changes on the Metro."

"Mmmm. I think it will be all right now that I'm used to it," Josephine murmured. "Maybe we'll find that it goes much faster on the way home."

She stared innocently up at Sophie, and Sophie giggled. "It's cheating if you use magic."

"Just a tiny bit. I would have done it on the way, but I was so wobbly I couldn't make it work. Magic's quite tricky, you know. Even for someone as naturally magical as a guinea pig." Josephine said this quite seriously, and Sophie struggled to keep a straight face. Even though she'd seen Josephine and Angelique use a little pinch of magic here and there, the very idea of magical guinea pigs still made her laugh.

"Sophie, come on, let's go and buy our tickets," Mum called, and Sophie hurried over to her.

"It's this way, Mum, down these steps. Look, I can see the boats!"

"So can I. Oh, Sophie. . ." Mum stopped, holding on to the railing and looking at the water.

"What's the matter?" Sophie ran back up the steps, looking at her anxiously.

"Your mother has gone a very interesting shade of green. . ." Josephine whispered from inside Sophie's bag.

"Mum, are you OK? You look like you might be sick. Do you want to sit down?" Sophie gently pulled her mum down the steps to sit on a bench. "What's the matter?"

Mum slumped on to the bench, and pressed her hand over her mouth for a moment. "Oh, Sophie, I'm so sorry," she said at last. "I thought it was going to be OK, but I just can't..."

"Can't what?" Sophie asked, surprised.

"Boats . . . I just can't do it, Sophie. They make me sick. I really thought I'd be all right on a big trip boat like that, but then I saw it. Even just thinking about getting on to it, I came over all funny. I'm so sorry, darling, I know you really wanted to go on a boat trip."

Sophie swallowed hard. She had been so excited about their trip on the river, she hated to think that now they wouldn't be able to go at all. But Mum looked awful – really pale and wobbly. "It doesn't matter," she said, patting Mum's hand. "Honestly. It's fine." She slipped her other hand inside her bag to give

Josephine an apologetic stroke.

"Don't worry!" It was the faintest whisper.

"Perhaps we could go up the *Tour Eiffel* instead?" Mum suggested. "Would you like that? There's an amazing view."

Sophie looked thoughtful. She didn't think Mum was up for climbing all those steps, even if she pretended she was fine. "If you know that you don't actually have to go on one, do boats still make you feel sick?" she asked slowly.

"No . . . I don't think so."

"Would it be all right if we just sat here and watched them all go by, then? It's so nice sitting by the water. We can wave to the people on the boats. And there are all the houseboats to look at too."

Mum nodded slowly. "Yeeesss. But I might just close my eyes for a minute, until I feel better. I really am sorry, Sophie. This doesn't feel like much of a fun day out for you. Give me just a few minutes to recover and we'll go and find something else fun to do, I promise. Just stay close by, Sophie, won't you?" She shut her eyes and leaned back against the bench. Sophie watched her for a moment, and then cautiously opened her bag, so that Josephine could hop out.

"No one will notice you if you keep

still," she
whispered.
"They'll just
think you're a
toy, like Mum
does."

Josephine
clambered on to
Sophie's lap and
sat down, leaning against Sophie's tummy
and sticking out her back legs to try and
look like a teddy bear.

They sat there in the autumn sunshine,
lazily watching the boats drift by, and
then Josephine tapped Sophie's hand. "I
think your mother is asleep."

Sophie peered over. "You're right! Oh dear, poor Mum. She's been working so hard recently. She stays up really late to get everything done." She looked hopefully towards the river and the moored houseboats. "She said to stay close, but if we didn't go very far, perhaps we could go and have a little look at the boats. Don't you think?"

"Oh, yes. . ." Josephine nodded seriously. "After all, if we sit here and talk, we might wake up your poor *maman*. And she needs her sleep, she isn't well. It's our *duty* to go for a walk."

"Come on, then." Quietly, they crept away from the bench and over to the edge of the water. There they stood, with Josephine tucked in Sophie's arms, watching the glittering ripples as a boat glided by.

"It's perfect," Sophie whispered.

Chapter Four

Sophie walked a little further along the
riverbank – not too far, she could still see
Mum, snoozing on her bench. She could
dash back as soon as Mum looked as if she
was waking up.

"They're like little houses," Josephine
breathed delightedly, as they wandered

along beside the moored boats. "Look, this one has flowers on the top. And a herb garden!"

The boats were beautiful, with gleaming paintwork and shining brass portholes along the sides. A few even had tables and chairs set out on the decks so the owners could eat their lunch outdoors and watch the river.

"Wouldn't it be fun to live on a boat?" Sophie sighed enviously. "If you were bored, you could just pull up your anchor and sail away. You'd just have to float down the river until you found somewhere else nice to stay."

"I wonder if there are guinea pigs on the river anywhere? Do you think we're the only ones, Sophie?"

"I've never heard of any others," Sophie said slowly. "But then I wouldn't have believed there were guinea pigs under *Sacré Coeur* until a few weeks ago. Perhaps there are colonies all over the place!"

At this point a delicate cough sounded from below the promenade, and Sophie and Josephine stared at each other in surprise. "Did you hear...?" Sophie whispered, and Josephine nodded, her eyes wider and rounder than ever.

"Do you think it's another guinea pig?" she hissed. "A river pig!"

"Maybe." Sophie crouched down, and she was just going to lean over the edge of the promenade to look, when a neat little red-brown face appeared over the side, peering at her with dark, sparkling eyes. His head was about the same size as Josephine's, and he had the same sort of small rounded ears, but he definitely wasn't a guinea pig.

"Morning!"

"Er, hello..." Sophie tried to smile, but she was so surprised to see another talking creature in the city that she couldn't think of anything friendly to say. *What are you?* sounded so rude.

The animal – whatever he was – scrambled further up the side of the wall, and turned out to have a white chin and front, rather smeared with dark oily

marks, white paws and a long back. He
was wearing a tattered blue scarf around
his neck, and there was a greasy cap on the
very back of his head. He had a little brown
brush of a tail and a cheeky grin.

"I know!" Sophie said suddenly. "I
remember. You're a stoat. Isn't that right?"

She said it in English – she didn't know the
word in French – and the animal looked
politely enquiring, as though he didn't
know either.

Sophie frowned at Josephine, wishing
her French was better. But she'd never
thought of asking Mum for the word for
stoat. "Do you know what he is?" she asked
hopefully. "I think I do, but I can't think of
the proper word."

"Ummm, *une hermine*?" Josephine
suggested, looking at him with her head on
one side.

"*Non*! I most certainly am not. Tch."

For a moment, Sophie thought he was
going to disappear over the side of the

promenade again, he was so insulted. But perhaps he was as curious about Sophie and Josephine as they were about him, as he simply folded his paws and glared. *"Je ne suis pas une hermine. Je suis une belette."* Then in strongly accented English, he added, "I am a *weasel*. Not a stoat. Pah!"

"A weasel!" Sophie shook her head apologetically. "I'm sorry, I don't think I've ever seen a real weasel before. Are you very rare?"

The weasel looked rather shocked, and then pleased. "Oh, yes, most definitely. Very unusual."

Josephine was looking backwards and forwards between them rather worriedly, the way Sophie did when her mum talked French very fast to her friends. Sophie had taught the guinea pig some English words, but they usually spoke French to each other.

"I should have known," Sophie told him. "It's my dad's favourite joke. I don't know if you'll understand it, even though your English is very, very good."

"I try," the weasel said modestly. "We sailors, we learn a great many languages. I myself can talk in six, you know. Tell me this joke."

"I don't think it's all that funny, but my dad starts laughing as soon as he tries to tell it. It goes like this. How do you tell the

difference between a stoat and a weasel?"

"Huh. Well, a stoat is about ten centimetres longer and he has a dark tip on the end of his tail. And besides, they're all ugly, bad-tempered so-and-sos." The weasel shook his head. "You're right, it isn't funny."

"No, no, that isn't the joke, I haven't got to the joke yet." Sophie took a deep breath. "A weasel is weaselly recognizable but a stoat is stoatally different."

The weasel frowned, and repeated it to himself under his breath. Then he suddenly started to laugh. "Aha! Ahahahahaha! Weaselly rrrrecognizable! Ahahahaha!" Then he fell off the edge of the promenade because he was laughing so much.

"Oh, no!" Sophie squeaked. "Oh, no, Josephine! He'll drown!"

But the weasel was still laughing, lying on his back in a tiny boat, slapping his paw against the side and growling, "Weaselly rrrrecognizable!" to himself over and over again.

"It's all right." Sophie let out a sigh of relief. "He landed in his boat. That was lucky." She was back to speaking French now, so that Josephine could understand.

"He has a boat?" Josephine scrambled out of Sophie's arms so she could look too. She kneeled at the very edge of the promenade and leaned over. "Oh! What a very smart boat!"

"I made her myself," the weasel told Josephine, straightening himself out. He stood up and waved a flourishing paw at the dinghy. "She used to be a fruit crate, you know. She smells of strawberries, on a warm day. That's why I named her *The Saucy Strawberry*."

The boat was still mostly box-shaped, but she had oars, and smart padded benches for the rower and his guests. The holes in the wooden fruit crate had been covered with more pieces of wood, nailed on, and there was a pointed prow attached to the front, with a tiny flagpole.

"She is beautiful," Josephine told him.

"I wish my sister Angelique could see her – she is a very clever builder of things too."

"Would you like to take a trip down the river?" the weasel asked, looking rather pleased. Then he bowed his head to Sophie. *"Je suis désolé, Mademoiselle.* I am so sorry, but I do not think you will fit."

"I definitely wouldn't." Sophie smiled at him. "That's all right. I'll run along the bank and watch you. Do you live in this boat, *Monsieur?"*

"No, no. I live in the houseboat, here." The weasel waved at the large boat that towered above his tiny craft. "The old man who owns it is a bit frail – not up to looking after everything. I help him out. There's lots of jobs on a boat that are best done by someone weasel-sized."

"Does he know that you're there?" Josephine asked curiously. "Shouldn't you be a secret? My sister was furious with me when I told Sophie about us."

The weasel wrinkled his muzzle, creasing the fur. "He does and he doesn't. If you asked him about the weasel living on his boat, he'd give you a funny look. But he knows that there's someone around handing him the right tools. Sorting out that strange clanking noise the engine's making before he gets to it. Every so often of an evening he'll be sitting up on deck, drinking his coffee, and I'll come and sit close by. He can tell there's someone there. He gives me biscuits."

"What's your name?" Sophie asked suddenly. "We don't know your name! I'm Sophie and this is Josephine."

"Diesel Weasel." A small paw reached up over the edge of the promenade and the weasel shook Sophie's finger, and then Josephine's paw. "That's what everyone calls me. You get to smell of diesel a bit, when you're always in and out of a boat engine."

"It's a very good name." Sophie smiled.

"It fits you perfectly."

"*Merci beaucoup*." The weasel nodded graciously. "So, *Mademoiselle*. Would you like to travel on the river?"

Josephine looked up at Sophie, her eyes troubled. "We were going to have an adventure together," she murmured.

"It doesn't matter! It's still an adventure for me too – I'll be right beside you." Sophie looked back up at the bench. "Mum's still asleep and we won't be long. We won't, will we?" she added to the weasel. "We promised not to go too far."

"No, no. A short trip only. Perhaps along the river as far as the beautiful cathedral of *Notre-Dame*?"

"Oh, yes! I would love to see that," Josephine agreed. "I could tell Angelique about it."

"Very well, then. All aboard!"

Chapter Five

Sophie raced along the edge of the
river, waving to Josephine in *The Saucy
Strawberry*. Josephine was dancing from
one side of the little boat to the other,
peering over the sides into the water, then
stopping to stare up at the view of Paris
floating by. She kept clapping her paws

with excitement. Every so often she would squeak to Sophie. "Look! Look how tall the *Tour Eiffel* is! It's enormous from down here on the water, Sophie! Oh, oh, another boat!"

Even though the Seine was calm, the dark water just sparkling a little in the sunshine, *The Saucy Strawberry* bounced about quite a lot. Whenever one of the trip

boats went by, Diesel Weasel's little craft
surged up and down on its wake, the great
long ripples hitting the boat like waves.

Sophie shivered, thinking of poor
Mum. If she'd been on a boat, she would
definitely have been sick. Sophie had
a feeling she might have been too. But
Josephine was delighted and didn't look in
the least bit seasick.

Diesel Weasel stopped rowing for a
moment and shipped his oars so as
to point something out to Josephine.
Sophie couldn't hear what he said,
but then Josephine waved wildly at
her. Her loud squeaks echoed over
the water. "Sophie! Look over there!

It's the cathedral! *Notre-Dame!*"

Sophie had seen lots of pictures of *Notre-Dame* – it was Paris's most famous church, nearly seven hundred years old. And Mum had taken her and Dan to visit it soon after they'd arrived in Paris. But Sophie had found it hard to see the cathedral properly with all the visitors milling around. It was surrounded by tall houses and shops too, so Sophie had felt as if it crept up on her. It was just suddenly there, big and grey and looming over her head. She hadn't thought it was as beautiful as everyone said it would be.

Now, from down here by the water, it felt so different. The two great towers

shone golden-white in the sunlight, and between them was a window shaped like a flower. It made Sophie think of a palace in a fairy tale.

As they came closer to the cathedral, the river ran under a delicate cast iron bridge and Sophie dithered for a moment, wondering if she should dash up the steps and cross the bridge for a closer look. She'd like to see the side of the cathedral a bit better – there was another of those flower-shaped windows and this one was even bigger, glittering in shades of scarlet and blue. She didn't want to lose sight of Josephine and Diesel Weasel, though. Perhaps they could moor up and all go over the bridge together to look? Sophie turned round to wave at them and gasped.

Josephine and the weasel were admiring the cathedral too. Sophie could hear Josephine's squeaky little voice, floating across the water. "Oh, yes, it's very nice indeed. But, of course, I like my lovely church better. This one doesn't have enough domes. Just all those spiky bits."

It would have been funny, if it weren't for the great, dark shape spearing through the water towards the tiny, fragile *Strawberry*.

"Josephine! Look out!" Sophie screamed. "Look behind you! There's a – a thing!"

Josephine and Diesel Weasel turned

towards Sophie, and the weasel peered worriedly into the water.

"Where?" he called back to Sophie. "I can't see anything – did you mean that boat?" He pointed to a boat puttering slowly down the river.

"No! It wasn't a boat, it was *in* the water," Sophie wailed. "It was coming up underneath you. It was some sort of fish, but it was huge. Honestly." She held her hand up to shield her eyes from the bright sun, and tried to peer into the water. But there was nothing there. Perhaps she had imagined it, after all. Had it been the shadow of a tree, maybe? Or a piece of litter, swirling about in the water?

Then her breath caught in her throat, and she screamed again. "There it is! I can see it. Look, it's coming up behind you!"

There was a deeper shadow cutting through the dark green water, towards the Strawberry. A fish at least twice as long as the boat! As Sophie watched, the huge creature broke the surface of the water, jaws open, ready to strike.

"A pike! You're not having my *Strawberry*, you horrible creature!" Diesel Weasel leaped up and hit the huge creature over the head with one of his oars. "Take that, you toothy great lump!" he shouted, jumping up and down and whopping

the pike on the nose. "Get away! Pick on someone your own size."

The pike retreated, slipping away into the darkness of the water, and Josephine squeaked, "You did it! You saved us!" while Sophie clapped from the bank.

But Diesel Weasel shook his head. "No. He'll be back. They're persistent, pikes. Hungry." He shuddered. "And I've never seen one as big that. Abandon ship, *Mademoiselle*! Abandon ship! Ah, my poor little *Strawberry*, turned into toothpicks for a dirty great pike!"

"It's coming back?" Josephine asked faintly, clutching at the side of the boat. "Oh!"

"Now, listen to me," the weasel told her. "As soon as we get close enough to this boat here, we must jump, do you understand?" He pointed to the small boat that was coming up on their starboard side, and then he began to row towards it, with great strong pulls on the oars. "Reach out and grab the fenders, or that rope dangling there," he shouted.

Sophie watched, frozen with fear, as they prepared to clamber aboard.

Diesel Weasel sprang lightly on to one of the fenders slung over the side of the boat, and stretched down his paw to Josephine to help her.

The little guinea pig reached towards him – but there was a sudden swirl in the water as the pike surfaced again, this time just next to the *Strawberry*, and clear enough for Sophie to see. He was huge, almost snake-like, with a long, mottled greenish body and a heavy, pointed snout. Clearly he was hoping to lunge in and snatch the juicy guinea pig morsel.

The gap between the two boats suddenly widened and Josephine squealed as her paws slipped away from the weasel. Diesel

Weasel let out a shout of horror as he was carried away and Josephine was left behind, alone on the *Strawberry*.

There was a splintering sound as the pike sank its needle-sharp teeth into the side of the boat, tearing away a part of the hull.

"I'm sinking!" Josephine wailed. "The river's all in the boat!"

Chapter Six

Sophie looked around for a lifebelt, or something – anything – to throw to Josephine. But there was nothing. Hastily, she started to undo her shoes so she could jump into the water and save her.

"No, Sophie!" Josephine cried. "He'll eat you too!"

Sophie was almost sure that the pike wasn't big enough to eat a human – he could probably give her a nasty bite, though. But she couldn't let Josephine be eaten. "What about magic?" she called, as she struggled with her laces – why did they have to get knotted up just now? Perhaps she should just jump in with them on. She wasn't a brilliant swimmer, though, she wasn't sure she could swim with boots on. "Can't you magic yourself on to the bank, Josephine? You must be able to do something, please!"

Josephine shook her head. "Too cold, too damp, too scared!" she squeaked. "Goodbye, Sophie!" The slowly sinking boat twirled about as the pike made

another lunge at it, and it wobbled into the shadow of the bridge.

The bridge! Sophie let out a yelp of excitement and gave up on her laces. She bounded up the steps, hauling her scarf out of her bag, and raced for the far edge of the bridge. Then she crouched, reaching through the metal railings to dangle her long knitted scarf down to the water.

Would the little wooden boat come bobbing under the bridge? Sophie crossed her fingers, and wished. "Please, please let her be all right!"

And then there she was, a bedraggled little ginger-and-white guinea pig, perched on the top of the very last bit of sinking boat, holding her pink tutu out of the water with one paw, and the sailor hat on her head with the other.

"Josephine,

up here! Grab hold!" Sophie yelled.
"Quick, before he comes round again!"
She could see the pike, lazily circling the
boat, waiting for the guinea pig to fall into
his jaws.

Even though Sophie's scarf was very
long (she and her gran had knitted it
together, it had taken months and Sophie
loved it) it wasn't quite long enough to
reach all the way to the water, however
much she stretched. "Jump!"

Josephine stood on tiptoe as the last
corner of the boat disappeared beneath
the water, and sprang, tutu flapping as
she grabbed the trailing fringe of the scarf
with her claws.

Laughing in relief, Sophie began to haul up the scarf like a fishing line, with her catch dangling on the end. Josephine twirled round slowly on the scarf, holding on with all her claws.

At last, Sophie pulled her through the railings, and Josephine fell into her arms with a faint squeak and snuggled against her silently. Josephine was almost never silent, so Sophie could see how upset and frightened she was.

"What happened to Diesel Weasel?" she asked at last, in a small voice.

"Down here," came a low hiss from under the bridge, and they looked round to see the weasel hiding in the shadows

by the steps and waving to them. Sophie picked Josephine up and carried her down the steps to meet him.

"*Je suis désolé, Mademoiselle*," said the weasel, all of him drooping. "I never meant to put you in danger. And then to leave you behind, while I leaped to safety! I am truly ashamed of myself."

"You didn't mean to," Sophie said. "It was just that the pike came back at the wrong time and pulled the boat away."

"The captain should always go down with his ship," Diesel Weasel said glumly.

"Well, what would be the point of that?" Josephine stared at him. "Surely you can build a new boat, can't you? If you find another crate? You could call it the ... er ... *The Brilliant Banana*," she suggested helpfully, and Sophie started to laugh.

"What? I think it's a very good name!" Josephine said indignantly.

"Perhaps I could build another," said Diesel Weasel, tapping his chin with his paw. "With some additions! I could have a mast, and sails! That would have given us the speed to get away from that monster pike. Or perhaps a paddle wheel..." He nodded gratefully to Josephine. "Yes! And when I do, I will take you out on the river again," he promised.

"No!" Josephine squeaked. "I mean,

merci beaucoup, thank you very, very much, but no. I think I am a land creature, after all."

"Really?" The weasel stared at her, disappointed.

"She *was* almost eaten," Sophie pointed out.

"I suppose so." But the weasel still sounded doubtful.

"Wouldn't you be scared to go back on the water?" Josephine asked him. "What if that pike remembers you?"

"Pffft." The weasel waved a paw. "Pikes. Silly, fishy lumps. I'm not scared of pikes."

"He is *very* silly," Josephine whispered

to Sophie. "I think I've actually met someone who is less sensible than me, Sophie! I must tell Angelique."

"Yes. And, oh, we must get back to Mum!" Sophie gasped. "She'll be waking up – maybe she woke up ages ago. Here, let me wrap you in the scarf to keep you warm." She wound it all around the shivering guinea pig and carefully tucked Josephine into her bag. "Would you like a ride?" she asked the weasel politely.

"No, no . . . I shall go back along the promenade and keep an eye out for some likely boxes. A very great pleasure to meet you both. I do hope you change your mind about coming out on my new boat,

Miss Josephine. I shall make sure it's pike-proof!" He waved and then dashed away, darting in and out of the shadows to avoid the people walking along the side of the river.

"Hurry back, Sophie, we do not want to upset your *maman*," Josephine whispered. "Ooooh, this scarf is so very nice and warm. I do not like rivers, I have decided."

Sophie jogged along the promenade, hoping that Mum wouldn't be too worried about her. It seemed a much longer way back than it had been when she was following the *Strawberry*. She was out of breath by the time she saw the houseboats and the bench where they'd left Mum.

"She's gone!" she whispered worriedly to Josephine. "Oh, no! What if she's gone to find a policeman and reported me lost?"

"Behind you!" Josephine squeaked.

Sophie spun round and saw Mum waving to her.

"There you are! Were you looking at the boats? I'm so sorry, Sophie, I can't believe I slept for that long! I suppose it's all the work I've been doing. Were you terribly bored?"

Sophie swallowed a laugh. Bored! "No, it was all right. . . We – I mean I – walked along the promenade a little way. It's beautiful." Then she shivered. "But the water looks very deep. I saw a huge fish. . ."

"Oh, really?" Her mum nodded. "The Seine is full of wildlife now — it's much cleaner than it used to be. How exciting!"

Sophie nodded. It *had* been exciting — after all, Josephine had wanted an adventure. But perhaps it had been just a little bit too much of one. . .

"What about something nice to eat?" Mum suggested. "For a treat? Shall we go to a café and have hot chocolate and cake?"

Sophie felt her bag wriggle, and a little ginger-and-white face popped up next to her shoulder. "Cake!" Josephine whispered. "Oh, yes, Sophie! I'm still very shocked, you know, and terribly cold. I need sugar – and possibly cream. Don't you think?"

Sophie giggled. "Yes, please, Mum."

Have you read...

Furry FRIENDS

Sophie's Squeaky Surprise

HOLLY WEBB

Illustrated by Clare Elsom

Read on for a sneak peek!

CHAPTER ONE

Sophie peered out over the view, watching the sunlight sparkle on the windows, and wondering who lived there, under the roofs. She couldn't see her own house from here, or she didn't think she could, anyway. She hadn't lived in Paris for long enough to know.

The city *was* very beautiful, but it still
didn't feel like home. Sophie sighed, and
rested her chin on her hands. She missed
her old house, and her old bedroom, and
her cat, Oscar. Grandma was looking

after him while they lived in Paris, but Sophie was sure that Oscar missed her, almost as much as she missed him.

"What are you looking at?" Dan squashed up next to her, leaning over the stone balcony.

"Just things," Sophie said vaguely. "The view."

"Boring," Dan muttered. "This is taking ages. And I'm hungry." He turned round, holding his tummy in both hands and made a starving face at Sophie. His nose scrunched up like a rabbit's, and Sophie smirked. She crossed her eyes and poked her tongue out at the corner of her mouth to make Dan laugh. After all, even a wonderful view can be boring when you've been looking at it for a *VERY LONG TIME*.

All the people who live in Paris love their city so much, and many of them walk up the steep steps to the church on their wedding days to have their photographs taken next to the wonderful view. But it can take an awful long time to get the photographs right, especially when it's windy and your auntie's wedding dress won't stay still properly.

"Sophie and Dan! Stop making faces like that! You're making Dad giggle, and he's supposed to be taking romantic photos!" Mum glared at them, but Dad rolled his eyes, and stuck his tongue out at Dan. Sophie thought Dad might be a bit bored with the photos as well.

This church was one of Sophie's favourite places in Paris. It was so pretty, and there was the fountain to look at, and all the people. She even liked its name, *Sacré Coeur*, which meant Sacred Heart. Sophie thought it was very special to have a whole church that was all about love. Auntie Lou's wedding had been beautiful too, but Sophie had got up early for Mum to curl her hair and fuss over her dress, and she was tired of having to stand still and smile.

"Go and play," Auntie Lou suggested.

"Go and run around for a bit. You can come back and be in the photos later."

"Later?" Dad moaned. "I thought we'd nearly finished!" But Sophie and Dan were already halfway down the white marble steps, and couldn't hear him.

"I wish we'd brought a ball. . ." Dan said, as they stopped in front of the fountain that stood below the balcony. He was looking at the grassy slope of the hill. "Do you think Mum would mind if we went home and got one? It wouldn't take five minutes."

"Yes, she would! And anyway, even *you* couldn't play football on that grass," Sophie pointed out. "It would just roll down to the bottom."

"Exactly. That would make it more fun! Uphill football, I've just invented it. I might be famous!"

Sophie shook her head. "I don't think all the people taking photos would be very impressed either. There are loads of them. They'd tell you off."

"Huh." But Dan looked round at all the visitors, and realized Sophie was right. No one looked as if they wanted to play football. And there was an old lady sitting on the bench over there with a really pointy umbrella, the kind with a parrot's head handle. She looked like she'd happily use the pointy end to stab footballs, and even the parrot seemed to be giving him a fierce glare.

"Race you up and down the balustrades then!" He grabbed her hand and hurried her down the two flights of stairs to the path.

Sophie squirmed. The balustrades were the stone slopes at the sides of the steps. They were wide and flat, and Dan loved to run up and down them. He'd discovered the game the first time they came to visit the church, just after they'd moved to Paris, and since *Sacré Coeur* was on their way home from school, he'd been practising. But the game made Sophie feel sick, especially when it had been raining and the stone was all slick and slippery. She was sure that he would fall off.

"Come on, Sophie!" Dan hopped up to the stonework. "You get up on the other side. Bet I can beat you back to the top!"

Sophie stood on the bottom step, looking anxiously at the flat white slope. She didn't want to run up it — but if she refused, Dan would keep on and on teasing her.

"Baby!" her brother called scornfully, and Sophie scowled. She was only a year younger than Dan! She was not a baby! Carefully, the tip of her tongue sticking out between her teeth, she stepped on to the balustrade. It wasn't really so very high, after all. . . And Dan looked so surprised that she'd done it! Sophie grinned at him.

"Go!" Dan yelled, dashing away up the slope. Sophie gasped, and raced after him,

wishing she had trainers on, and not her
best shoes with the glittery bows.

She slithered a little, and gasped and
reached out her hands to balance,
wishing there was something to hold on
to – a tree maybe. But there was only
the perfect short green grass, and every

so often those funny little cone-shaped bushes that almost looked like upside-down ice creams.

Halfway to the top, Dan let out a yell as he spotted one of his friends from school on the other side of the hill. He hopped down and raced across the grass to see Benjamin, leaving Sophie glaring after him. He'd just abandoned their race, after she'd been brave enough to climb the balustrade at last. How could he? She folded her arms and tapped her foot crossly on the stone. Brothers! They were so rude!

If only she had a friend to play with, too. It wasn't fair. Sophie watched Dan

and Benjamin chasing each other across
the grass, and sighed sadly. Somehow,
she just hadn't found anybody she liked
that much at school yet. Even though
Mum had spoken French to them ever
since they were little, Sophie still felt
as though she wasn't doing it quite
right. The teachers told her she was
doing ever so well, but the girls in her
class looked at her funny whenever
she opened her mouth. And then they
just ran off. After some days at school,
Sophie wondered if she might forget
how to talk at all. It was nothing
like back home. Mum had suggested
sending emails to her friends from their

school in London, and Sophie had, but it wasn't the same at all. All the fun things that Elizabeth and Zara told her in their replies only made Sophie feel more left out.

The only girls who'd really spoken to her were Chloe and Adrienne, and that was because their teacher had asked them to look after the new girl. Sophie had decided halfway through the first morning that she'd much rather be unlooked-after. Chloe didn't do anything except twitch her nose and giggle, which was boring, though bearable, but Sophie thought

Adrienne was possibly the nastiest person she had ever met. Because her voice was so sweet and soft, the things she said sounded perfectly nice at first. It was only when Sophie thought back that she realized how horrible they actually were.

"So, why *did* you move here?" Adrienne had a way of looking at Sophie with her head on one side that made Sophie feel like she was some ugly sort of beetle.

"Your French is quite good. For an English person, I mean. . ."

"I suppose that's an *English* skirt. It's very . . . interesting."

Sophie gave a little shiver, even though the sun was warm on her bare shoulders. It was a hot September afternoon, but Adrienne's pretty voice was like cold water trickling down her spine, even when she was only remembering it.

She sighed again, and then shuddered as Dan and Benjamin started a race, rolling down the grassy slope.

And then she fell off.